For my father, Don,
and my son, Ingo
— C.R.

Phaidon Press Inc.
65 Bleecker Street
New York, NY 10012

Phaidon Press Limited
Regent's Wharf
All Saints Street
London N1 9PA

phaidon.com

First published 2019
© 2019 Phaidon Press Limited
Text and illustrations copyright © Chris Raschka
Text set in Aetna Regular and Aetna Condensed

ISBN 978 0 7148 7866 9
004-1218

A CIP catalogue record for this book is available from
the British Library and the Library of Congress.

Designed by Meagan Bennett

Printed in China

Side
by
Side

Chris Raschka

Horse

**and
rider**

Queen

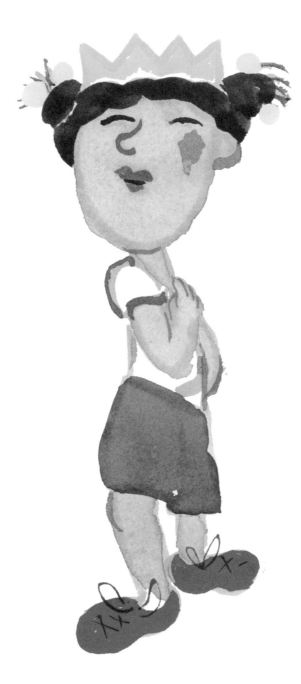

**and
jester**

Side by side

Crane

and cargo

Engine

and railcar

Side
by
side

Boat

and
captain

Base

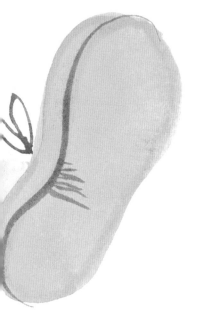

**and
explorer**

Side

by side

Side
by

by

by

by   side

side

side

side

by   side

Mountain

and climber

Dreamer

**and
doer**

Side

by side

Teacher

and learner

Learner

and teacher

Side
by
side

Bed
and sleeper

Sleeper
and waker

Today
and
tomorrow

Side
by
side

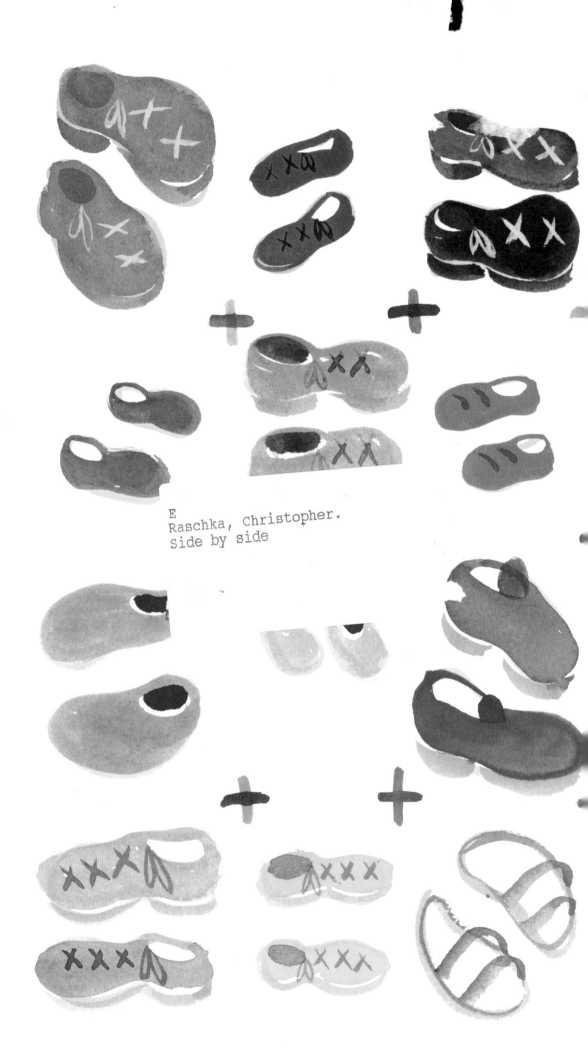